PING
AND THE
MISSING RING

EMMA SHEVAH

ILLUSTRATED BY
IZZY EVANS

BLOOMSBURY EDUCATION

BLOOMSBURY EDUCATION

Bloomsbury Publishing Plc
50 Bedford Square, London, WC1B 3DP, UK
29 Earlsfort Terrace, Dublin 2, Ireland

BLOOMSBURY, BLOOMSBURY EDUCATION and the Diana logo are trademarks
of Bloomsbury Publishing Plc

First published in Great Britain in 2021 by Bloomsbury Publishing Plc

A catalogue record for this book is available from the British Library

ISBN: PB: 978-1-4729-9409-7; ePDF: 978-1-4729-9411-0; ePub: 978-1-4729-9410-3

2 4 6 8 10 9 7 5 3 1

Cover and text design by Laura Neate

Printed and bound in the UK by CPI Group Ltd, CR0 4YY

To find out more about our authors and books visit www.bloomsbury.com and sign up
for our newsletters

CONTENTS

CHAPTER ONE
HALF TERM

Finally, the day had arrived. As Ping packed her suitcase, she was so excited she could barely speak. If she did, the words might burst from her mouth in a blast of heat, noise and energy, and that would not do at all. Not in Ping's family. You see, Ping and her family were Thai, and the custom for Thai people is to be calm, composed and polite. Typically, Thai people do not appreciate words bursting in blasts from people's mouths – even eager, excited words. Certainly not cross, cantankerous ones – that was not acceptable in the least. Whenever Ping spoke too quickly or too loudly, or when her tone turned as dark as a country road at night, her parents would frown a little and murmur, "Shh, shh, Ping. Please be calm, OK?"

Ping tried – she really did – but being calm was difficult. She seemed to have springs in her shoes, bubbles in her body, and roars and giggles and yells trying to leap free from her lungs to the tips of the trees. When she felt the bubbles rise and the giggles gather, she would firmly clamp a lid on top, but all too often it would rip off when she least expected it and whatever was inside her would explode outwards noisily. Now she was excited about the visit, it was almost impossible to keep the lid on.

"How are you getting on?" Ping's mother asked, drifting to Ping's bedroom door, her dark hair secured in a neat bun at the nape of her neck. Ping's mother, Chabah, seemed to glide rather than walk, as if she were a weightless cloud wafting over a warm current of air. She had once been a classical Thai dancer, and now she taught dance to students near their home. She moved elegantly and gracefully, as if she were always performing a slow, flowing dance to a mesmerised audience, but it was simply the dance of her life: the dance of slotting bills in her business folders, the dance of folding the laundry, the dance of paying for parcels at the Post Office. Ping liked how she moved her hands most of all. Even the way her mother washed an apple was poetic, gentle and unhurried, as though she were bathing, with the tenderest love and care, the head of a newborn baby.

Ping was getting on fine, in fact, so she nodded to keep the lid on. Her mother had already placed her clothes in a pile on the chair – all Ping needed to do was pack them. But then she just *had* to speak. "You were the last one to use the case!" she cried, almost erupting with delight at her genius detective work. She'd found a lone long black hair lying across the shell of the empty suitcase, and a single white trainer sock, unworn, in the zip pocket. In truth, it hadn't been difficult to work out – her mother had returned from a trip a few days ago and Ping had known she'd taken that particular suitcase because she'd seen it in the back of the car – but that didn't bother Ping. She was perfecting her powers of perception and honing her noticing skills, and she was definitely, *definitely* getting better.

Well, sort of. She hadn't noticed her father had moved the elephant painting from the hall to his study until her mother had asked him where it was, and she hadn't noticed her mother's haircut until Yai, her grandmother, had said it looked nice. But no one could expect Ping to be an expert: she'd only just started. And anyway, even genius detectives missed *some* clues. Didn't they?

Course they did. Missing the odd clue didn't matter.

Ping held out the trainer sock and her mother took it with a smile. She was wearing the dress Ping liked best, made of soft, shiny silk in a deep burnished orange with long diamonds of dark green, brown and gold. It was in a traditional Thai style, the skirt long and straight, and the top crossed at the front with bigger diamonds across the sleeves to match the hem of the skirt. In that dress, Ping thought her mother looked and moved like a rare, majestic green and orange butterfly. Ping hoped to be exactly like her mother when she grew up, but Ping's shoulder-length hair never looked neat, her clothes always seemed rumpled as if she'd slept in a hedge, and she did not look like or move like a butterfly. More like a hippopotamus.

Thinking of that made the bubbles surge and the giggles gather, but Ping kept them in.

"Fifteen minutes, OK?" her mother added. "Daddy's working so I'll drive you."

Ping nodded. Her father, Tui, worked in an office doing something that Ping couldn't quite fathom, involving numbers and graphs and budgets. He too was as serene as a stream of spring water. Even when the graphs caused his forehead to furrow, he spoke quietly and respectfully to all. He often travelled for business, and that was the reason Ping was going to stay with her cousins for half term: her father was travelling abroad, and her mother was teaching and performing Thai classical dance in London for the week.

Ping squeezed and squashed the last of her clothes in the case, feeling elated. She loved staying there. She loved Aunty Lek's home and she loved her cooking. She loved Aunty Lek's shop, which was like a treasure trove. She especially loved seeing her cousins, Tong and Taptim. And to top it all they had a new dog, which is why Ping had to keep her lips tightly zipped and her excitement tucked deep inside her, even though it bubbled up now and then, making her smile turn to a giggle.

Ping stood, scanned her room, and gathered more items she might need. A magnifying glass. A notebook and a pen. A small paintbrush for finding fingerprints. Not that she really knew how to find fingerprints, or why a paintbrush might be useful.

"Ready?" her mother asked, returning and casting her eye over the contents of Ping's open suitcase. Ping noticed her mother wince slightly but neither mentioned the slapdash packing or the somewhat crumpled suitcase contents.

Relieved, Ping nodded.

"Books?" Ping's mum asked. "Read two chapters every evening."

Ping nodded.

"Toothbrush? The card game you wanted to play with Taptim?"

Ping nodded.

"Good," her mother said, and performed the slow, gentle dance of patting down, then zipping up, the suitcase. "Best behaviour," she added.

Ping nodded.

"No shouting or... commotion."

Ping shook her head.

"Do what Aunty Lek asks."

Ping nodded.

"And no adventures."

Ping stretched her mouth so her heart-shaped lips looked as straight as a railway line. She and Taptim had dug deep holes in the garden one year, hoping to catch sight of Australia. Another year, she and Tong had chased a squirrel into the woods near the park and Aunty Lek had lost them for over half an hour. Last year, Taptim and Ping had walked to the corner shop, and instead of going straight home, they had detoured at the zebra crossing and raced to the swings and slides, causing Aunty Lek to worry and rush out in her car to search for them.

"No adventures, Ping," her mother repeated.

Ping shook her hesitant head.

"Say it, please."

Ping swallowed hard to suppress the bubbles. "No adventures. I will be extremely well behaved."

"Good," her mother replied. "If you are, we'll visit the alpacas when you come home."

Ping's eyes lit up. The bubbles bumped and boomeranged. The yells swelled and the giggles gathered. The alpacas! They lived on a farm nearby but she hadn't seen them for *ages*. She'd thought to name her favourite dark brown one 'Mr Al Packington' but perhaps he'd like 'Alberto Pacolito' more. She wanted to say each name to him aloud to check which he preferred, and to do that, she had to go and visit him.

She was even more excited now! Ping tried not to squeal, though her mouth wanted to. She tried not to jump up and down, though her body wanted to. And she tried not to run down the stairs, though her legs wanted to. When she reached the front door, she lifted her shoes from the shoe stand and tried to force her feet in without untying the laces, which always squashed the backs down.

"Ping Ping," her mother murmured, sliding on her slip-on shoes effortlessly. "Untie them, please."

Ping remembered the alpacas. She nodded, untied the yellow laces and put her shoes on properly, even though it took three times as long and made her insides itchy with impatience. Her mother wheeled the suitcase to the car and Ping climbed into the back seat, trying to keep the bubbles at bay as they pulled out of the driveway.

She would be beautifully, perfectly, gloriously behaved.

No adventures. Not even one.

CHAPTER TWO
AUNTY LEK'S HOUSE

Ping knew they'd arrived when the car crunched across the gravel of the driveway. Aunty Lek and Uncle Jip's white house wasn't far away: Richmond was only two hours from Ping's home in Bath, but their parents were so busy, Ping didn't see her cousins as much as she'd have liked. Their house, like Ping's, was on a wide, leafy street. It had pots of pink flowers flanking the driveway, angular bedrooms built into the loft, and a small summer house at the end of the garden, which Tong, Taptim and Ping used as their secret headquarters.

When the car came to a standstill, Ping threw open the door and leapt out. Seeing her mother's head turn slowly to look at her, Ping decided against sprinting, shrieking, to the door, her arms windmilling and her hair in her face, and instead walked as smoothly and quickly as her legs could scissor, her feet *crunch crunch crunching* across the gravel. It always sounded to her like a monster eating a handful of colossal crisps with its mouth open. Ping always wondered how her mother, who was bigger than Ping, sounded so much lighter when she walked, as if the monster was eating just one corner of a crisp with its mouth closed.

Butterfly, thought Ping, *and hippopotamus. That must be it.*

"*Sawasdee ka.*" Aunty Lek stood smiling at the door. She was Ping's father's sister and Ping thought she looked just like him.

Aunty Lek, Ping and Chabah placed their hands together in a *wai* and lowered their heads. Ping's *wai* was lower and deeper than her mother's as she was well aware she needed to show respect for her elders. Chabah and Aunty Lek spoke to each other in quiet voices with lots of smiles. Ping, on the other hand, tried not to burst into a billion pieces as her eyes darted from here to there in search of her cousins.

"So beautiful," Aunty Lek said approvingly, complimenting Chabah's dress. "Lovely colours."

Ping was too fidgety to care about clothes, but she knew she had to notice things even when she was excited – especially when she was excited because that's when she was least perceptive. So she breathed deeply, her nostrils whistling slightly, and noticed Aunty Lek was wearing a dark red shirt and wide black trousers stopping just below the knee. She noticed Aunty Lek's nails were painted the same deep red hue as her shirt and that Aunty Lek looked different, but Ping couldn't tell why.

"My, you've grown, Ping!" Aunty Lek said, but Ping didn't think she had at all. She was still smaller than all her friends. They seemed to drink a growth potion for breakfast instead of orange juice. Ping was still working out what was different about Aunty Lek when her mother said, "Ooh, your hair is lovely. Lighter, no?"

Her hair! That was it!

Ping frowned. She hadn't noticed Aunty Lek's was lighter, and that bothered her. What kind of detective didn't notice easy clues like that?

Aunty Lek nodded. "Had it done this morning. My nails, too. Jip's company has a dinner this evening. Not sure about my hair. Still getting used to it."

Annoyed with herself, Ping stepped over the entrance. Her bubbles of glee had almost popped, and the last wobbly, half-squished ones couldn't escape in an eruption because she couldn't see Tong, Taptim or Jelly anywhere.

"They've taken Jelly around the block," Aunty Lek explained. "Back soon."

Ping was bitterly disappointed. Why hadn't they waited for her? She would've *loved* to have taken Jelly for a walk. Now she had to wait for them to come back with her insides itching and her joy jagged, crumpled and crushed. She didn't even feel like noticing, and she *always* felt like noticing.

Ping's mum Chabah slipped off her shoes at the door. Ping wanted to lever hers off without untying the laces, but she remembered Mr Al Packington's funny face – or was it Alberto Pacolito? – and she sat down to untie them instead. She placed them precariously on the shoe rack and Aunty Lek pointed to some white towelling ones for guests. "Slippers?" she asked. Ping smiled politely and shook her head. She preferred wearing socks in Aunty Lek's house: the shiny wooden floors were excellent for sliding, though she had to make sure her mother wasn't looking when she did it.

There were other reasons Ping liked the house. Everywhere she looked, she was surrounded by Thai handicrafts, art and furniture – much more than they had in Ping's house. On the shelves were small ornate pots with pointed lids, and jars and teacups painted in gold, blue and green patterns. The glass-doored cabinets displayed small figures carved from wood, knick-knacks from markets and cloth dolls with top knots – handmade by hill people in the north. On the walls were brown and gold paintings of Thai villages in the old times, with wooden, pointy-roofed houses on stilts and villagers going about their daily chores wearing simple cloth wraps, their hair short and flat on top of their heads. A teak coffee table with elephants carved into the legs sat beside wide, cream-coloured sofas with cushion covers made of traditional prints matching the colours in the rugs and curtains.

Aunty Lek owned a shop selling Thai handicrafts and furniture. She travelled to Thailand often to ship things back, and now that her shop was busier, her cousin in Bangkok sent shipments too. Aunty Lek kept some of the most beautiful things for her home, and Ping loved it there.

Crunch crunch crunch crunch crunch.

Finally! Ping tried to keep the bubbles at bay as Aunty Lek opened the door and a brown and white bundle of energy charged in alongside her cousins.

Tong and Taptim greeted Ping's mum Chabah with a *wai* and then, as if banshees had been unleashed, Taptim and Ping ran to each other shrieking, hugging each other in a tangle of arms and jumping up and down.

"Shh, shh, girls," Chabah said, with a friendly frown. "Please be calm, OK?"

Taptim and Ping unhooked themselves, grinning. Growing up in Britain meant they had two cultures, not one. Sometimes the two worked well together, and sometimes they didn't. When they didn't, it became complicated and Ping felt torn, but she did like being able to move between them sometimes.

Taptim had changed. Ping noticed she had spots near her nose, which meant she was turning into a teenager a year too early, and might become grumpy quite soon. She had her hair tied high and wore neat black jeans, a short blue T-shirt and a black choker that seemed to be made of lace.

"You look old!" Ping laughed. She craned her neck to look up at Tong. "And you got so tall!" Tong stood back and didn't hug her: he was thirteen now and regarded her in a vaguely amused and vaguely bored way. His hair flicked and almost covered one of his eyes, and around his neck were wireless headphones. Ping thought it was funny that Tong was trying to be cool, but she secretly wished he was going to be the same Tong who played pranks on them, raised tadpoles in a tank until they were frogs, and tried to teach Ping to whistle using two fingers (though she still couldn't do it). He must have grown a head taller since she last saw him. "Lanky," she giggled. "Like someone stretched you in a pasta machine."

"You still look like a little bird," Tong replied with a wry smile, his voice sounding very odd. "But one that crashes into things and breaks them."

Ping grinned. It was true. That hippopotamus energy had a lot to answer for. Just then, Jelly jumped up on her legs and she rubbed his ears, laughing. He had as much energy as Ping did and seemed just as clumsy because he ran into the shoe rack, knocking the shoes off it and scattering them across the hallway.

"You'll met my new friend today," Taptim said. "I've met her in the shop a few times but she hasn't come to our house before." She scrolled on her phone and showed Ping a photo of a white dog.

"Your new friend is a dog?" Ping asked.

Taptim pointed at the girl shape behind the dog. "Noooo. Clementine. That's her dog, Spark. She's bringing him today. Mum said it was fine."

Foamy froth fizzled in Ping, but she kept the lid on. She *loved* dogs. And now there'd be two of them! Even better.

"You can be friends with Clementine as well," Taptim added, tucking her phone in her back pocket, "but if Spark likes you more than me, you'll have to sleep in the summer house."

Ping's expression changed to one of horror.

Taptim's laugh was more like a snort. "Your face! Hahaha."

When Ping's mum asked Tong about school, Ping noticed his voice again. It went from being high-pitched like a boy's to deep like a man's and then high like a boy's again. Was he doing it on purpose? Was he speak-yodelling? Ping wanted to laugh, but his expression was perfectly serious and her mother didn't seem confused in the least. Ping decided to ask Taptim about it later.

"Come and sit down," Aunty Lek said. The round table, covered with a pretty cotton tablecloth, was laden with plates of fruit: yellow, slippery mango; spiky-shelled rambutan; peeled, eyeball-like lychees; white, pulpy dragon fruit speckled with small black dots; and cold, orange melon cut into cubes. Aunty Lek always had the prettiest plates and bowls. Even the water glasses were dotted with tiny glass balls in the shape of flowers.

"Tea?" Aunty Lek asked in Thai, adding the short word *ka* that women said at the end of their sentences to be polite. Men said *krup* but it sounded more like 'cup' to Ping. Chabah nodded, and they spoke in Thai about Aunty Lek's shop, some new pieces she'd bought, and Isabelle, the new worker she had hired. Tong, Taptim and Ping politely ate fruit but Ping kept fidgeting, desperately wanting to run around with Jelly.

When her mother said goodbye, she squinted dubiously and reminded Ping, "No adventures, OK?"

Ping nodded with her serious face. "No adventures. See you in a week."

CHAPTER THREE
CLEMENTINE

Once the car had crunched away, Tong went to his room, and Ping and Taptim raced upstairs to unpack Ping's case and chat. Ping had six months of news and TV shows to discuss in great detail, and now that Taptim had put her phone away, Ping wanted to seize the moment. Taptim seemed to check it every five minutes, even though nothing had happened since the last time she had looked.

When Aunty Lek called them down an hour later, they ogled the unpacked suitcase with wide eyes. "Later," Taptim said. "Clementine's coming." She picked up her phone, checked it again, and then they skipped downstairs.

Rummaging noises were coming from what used to be the playroom. Ping peeped in and saw Aunty Lek surrounded by cardboard boxes of all shapes and sizes, and furniture and paintings covered in bubble wrap. "Wow," Ping said, her eyes scanning the room. "I've never seen it this full."

"Just had a delivery," Aunty Lek explained, gazing at it all anxiously. "The shop's been so busy, and now we're selling online, we've ordered more stock than ever. Sue – you've met Sue – she only works part-time, which is why I've employed Isabelle." Aunty Lek's head tilted as she heard a crunching noise. "That'll be her now. She's coming to help me sort this out." Aunty Lek washed her dusty hands, asked Taptim to put Jelly's lead on so he wouldn't run into the road, and opened the front door.

A long green estate car with one light blue door sat in the driveway. Ping noticed a cheerful white woman with curly red hair, freckles and a warm smile waving from the driver's seat. A girl with the same hair and even more freckles than her mother sat in the back holding the collar of a white dog with floppy ears.

"Clementine!" Taptim said with glee. "Spark!"

Jelly barked excitedly as Isabelle, Clementine and Spark got out of the car. Spark immediately ran in circles, twisting the lead around Clementine's legs and making everyone laugh. Ping noticed Isabelle's loose blue dungarees and flat pink trainers, and she noticed Clementine wore blue jeans with purple pom poms at the hem, a yellow and orange top, a shiny silver jacket and gold and blue shoes. *So many colours!* thought Ping, who liked her immediately.

Aunty Lek didn't *wai* to Isabelle – they just said hello, and then Isabelle put out her hand to shake Ping's. "Hello! We haven't met. I'm Isabelle and this is Clementine. Lovely to meet you." She shook Ping's hand decisively and Ping, thinking it was very adult and very English, wanted to giggle.

"I'm Ping," she grinned, wondering whether Clementine would shake her hand too, but Clementine didn't. She unwrapped Spark's lead from her legs, then smiled broadly, showing a gap between her front teeth. "He needs to… you know," Clementine said, nodding to the main road and laughing. "Long journey."

"We'll come!" Taptim tugged Jelly's lead and they followed Clementine.

Ping didn't move. "Does this count as an adventure?" she asked, checking.

"Err… we're going to the corner of the driveway," Taptim replied. "Not exactly an adventure, Ping." With a flick of her ponytail, she and Jelly crunched across the gravel, causing the monster to munch his crisps in a most rambunctious manner.

Relieved that driveway-dog-walks didn't count, Ping ran to her new friends – the one with two legs, and the one with four.

"I wish I could have a dog," Ping said, admiring Spark's floppy ears and untamed bounce. "He's so cute."

"Jelly, too," Clementine replied, her face flushing as Spark watered the tree. "What kind of dog is he?"

"Beagle," Taptim explained. "Excellent detective dog."

"Huuugghhh. Really?" Ping tickled behind Jelly's ears. "Perfect! He can help us solve mysteries."

"Shame we don't have any to solve," Taptim replied, and she turned towards the house.

But Taptim was wrong. A mystery was heading their way, and they would need all the help they could get. Canine included.

*

At the front door, Ping noticed that Clementine stepped on the entrance and not over it. Ping also noticed that Clementine didn't take off her shoes when she went in, even though Ping and Taptim did. Ping looked at Taptim, and Taptim looked at Ping, but neither of them said anything.

Isabelle did, though. She had been chatting to Aunty Lek in the hallway, and then said, "Excuse me, Lek – sorry." She pointed to the shoe rack inside the door and added, "Shoes, Clemmie."

"Oh." Clementine looked at everyone else's socked feet. "Why do you take your shoes off in the house?"

"So we don't bring dirt in," Isabelle explained. "Shoes are dirty – we wear them outside."

"But *we* don't do that," Clementine said, brightly.

31

"No, we don't, do we?" Isabelle smiled. "Maybe we should. Anyway, it's the right thing to do in a Thai house so please take them off."

Ping noticed Clementine didn't sit down to remove her shoes: she used a wall to balance, then held the back of one shoe with the toes of the other and forced it off without untying it. She switched feet, this time using her socked toes to lever her other shoe off. Isabelle didn't correct or scold her – she just put Clementine's shoes on the rack next to the others. Ping noticed the backs of Clementine's shoes were also squashed down from forcing her feet in, which made her smile. And she noticed that Clementine's socks didn't match: one had blue stars and the other pink stripes. There was plenty to notice about Clementine. She was *interesting*.

"Slippers?" Aunty Lek pointing to a pair on the stand.

Clementine looked from Ping's feet to Taptim's. "I'll just wear my socks," she said with a grin.

"Thank you so much for inviting us to lunch," Isabelle said, warmly. "I LOVE Thai food." She fished in her large canvas handbag and handed Aunty Lek a small square gift wrapped in silver paper. *Probably chocolates*, Ping thought, *or maybe a scarf in a box*. Her mother always gave scarves as gifts.

"Ohhhh, not necessary – but thank you," Aunty Lek said, bowing slightly, and she put the gift, unopened, on the sideboard next to the basket where Uncle Jip kept his keys. "We'll have some lunch and then get to work. Clementine, do you like Thai food?"

Clementine tilted her head. Ping thought she looked like an inquisitive bird. "I think so," she replied, thoughtfully. "But not too spicy."

"I haven't made it spicy today," Aunty Lek replied, smiling. "You have ten minutes to play with the dogs and then we'll eat."

Ping, Taptim and Clementine ran to the back door, slipped on some crocs, and lent a spare pair of very large red ones to Clementine. Ping was hoping to play with Jelly and Spark but they went on a sniffing expedition of the grass, so Taptim pointed at the summer house and said, "Meeting at HQ."

"What's HQ?" Clementine asked, clomping across the grass like a clown.

"Headquarters!" Taptim said over her shoulder as she ran off.

"Headquarters of what?" Clementine asked, turning to Ping.

"Our intelligence organisation," Ping replied with a wink. Clementine had more questions to ask, Ping could tell, but Taptim was at the door by then so they ran after her.

Clementine did indeed have questions and she asked them as soon as they sat on the cushioned benches inside.

"Am I doing this right?" she clapped her hands together hard, trying to *wai*, but her fingers were splayed open and her thumbs were sticking out.

Taptim and Ping giggled. "Not at all," Taptim said, and showed Clementine how to do it. "Press your hands together gently, don't slap them. Your wrists should be here, above your solar plexus, and your fingers should be closed with your thumbs in. No, point your fingers up towards your face, not out. That's it. Now, lift your hand a bit and lower your head – not *that* much! Tips of your fingers near your nose. That's better!"

Clementine practised again and again, adding (as she still clapped and bowed her head too low and hard), "Why didn't your mum open our present?"

"We open them afterwards," Taptim answered. "Not in front of people. Not unless they want us to."

"Is that a Thailand tradition?" Clementine asked.

"A *Thai* tradition, yes," Ping corrected her. "Don't know why, though."

"I want to be Thai," Clementine decided, making them grin. "Teach me more."

Ping said, "Umm… we step over the threshold when going through an entrance door, not on it."

"Why?" Clementine asked.

"There's an old belief that a spirit lives in the threshold," Ping explained, and then added, "You shouldn't touch anyone's head. And don't point your feet at people. Disrespectful."

Clementine tucked her feet under the bench and Taptim nodded. "Don't shout or get angry," she added. "Try to always be polite."

"I *am* always polite," Clementine replied, confidently. "At least, I try to be. Mum said it's important. When my dad got ill, we put traffic cones outside our house to save a parking spot so he wouldn't have to walk far after his hospital visits. Our neighbours got angry and rude," Clementine went on, "because we blocked the space and they didn't like it. I wanted to be rude back but Mum told me we should see it from their point of view and be nice no matter what. Dad's in a wheelchair now and anyway, the council gave us a disabled parking bay, so the neighbours felt bad and apologised. I guess Mum was right."

Ping's throat had gone dry and her stomach felt knotted. "Is… your dad OK?" she asked.

"He's OK," Clementine said softly, almost whispering, and gave a shrug. "I hope so, anyway." She pursed her lips and added, "So. Do either of you know how to make friendship bracelets?"

Ping and Taptim shook their heads.

"I'll teach you. We're coming back on Wednesday so I'll bring some strings. We can make them for each other, if you like. It's easy."

Ping felt the bubbles bounce but at least she could run around the garden to release them this time. The three of them chased Jelly and Spark in circles until it was time for lunch.

That afternoon, Aunty Lek and Isabelle spent hours in the storeroom. Ping, Taptim and Clementine talked endlessly, watched TV, ate ice cream and tried to teach the dogs to roll over. Before they left, Isabelle filled her water bottle in the kitchen for the journey home, then she and Clementine waved goodbye and they were gone.

"I can't *wait* 'til Wednesday," Taptim said. "She's so nice, isn't she?"

Ping nodded. "I think she's the nicest person I've ever met."

"Except me," Taptim said.

"Except you," Ping agreed. Even though she wasn't so sure.

CHAPTER FOUR
THE RING

Half an hour later, Aunty Lek came into the sitting room with her forehead wrinkled.

"Girls, have you... you haven't seen my engagement ring, have you? It was in the green dish – the one on the windowsill above the kitchen sink. The one I always wear here," she held up her bare left hand and wiggled a finger.

Taptim and Ping stopped playing cards and shook their heads.

"Strange," she said. "I took it off to cook lunch. I always leave it in that dish when I'm cooking, but it wasn't there when I went to put it on later."

"Maybe it fell off in the storeroom?" Taptim suggested.

"Maybe it's *under* the dish?" Ping said. "Shall we help you look?"

"Yes… please. I'll ask Tong to help as well."

The four of them searched for over an hour. By then Uncle Jip was home, and he and Aunty Lek needed to leave for the evening.

"Are you sure you left it in here?" Uncle Jip asked as they stood in the kitchen.

"I must have. I always leave it there."

"So… where is it?"

"I don't know." She looked at Uncle Jip in an odd way. Ping tried to work out what the look meant, but she had no idea. Adults had lots of looks, and half of them were impossible to decode. When Aunty Lek opened the door to Ameena, the babysitter, she was wringing her hands anxiously.

"We need to leave soon. We'll have to look later," Uncle Jip said, and they went upstairs to change.

In Taptim's bedroom, Ping unpacked her suitcase, frowning. She was trying very hard to remember. Had she noticed the ring in the dish in the kitchen? Had she even noticed the dish?

Taptim was lying on her bed, scrolling through her phone. "Taptim," she said, waving her hand in front of the screen to get her attention. "Where do you think it is?"

"Tut. Stop!" Taptim said, pulling her phone away. "It'll turn up. Can't have gone far."

"What if it doesn't? I'm checking the kitchen again," Ping said, getting up.

Taptim stretched lazily on her bed. "We've already looked."

"I'm looking again."

Ping was on her way downstairs when she heard voices in Aunty Lek's bedroom. She stood at Taptim's bedroom door and tuned her ears to the conversation, but she had to creep a bit closer down the hallway to hear properly.

"Isabelle came over today," Aunty Lek said. Ping strained to hear. "She was telling me about her money troubles – her husband is sick – and then she filled her water bottle before she left."

"What are you saying?" Uncle Jip asked.

"She was in the kitchen on her own."

"You don't think she…" Uncle Jip began and then stopped.

Ping stumbled backwards and her hand shot over her mouth.

"Where else can it be?" Aunty Lek asked. "I'm certain I left it there. I always leave it there."

Ping wanted to run to tell Taptim but she didn't want to miss anything.

"Should we call the police?" Uncle Jip asked.

POLICE?

Ping's stomach dropped to her socks.

"I don't have proof," Aunty Lek said. "But I tell you one thing, I can't work with someone I don't trust – or have her in our house again. I'll call her tomorrow and ask her not to come back."

Ping felt cold and faint. With her mouth hanging open she raced across the hall to tell Taptim. To her credit, Taptim put her phone down. "WHAT?" she mouthed once Ping

42

had squeaked, blurted and jabbered what she'd overheard.

"Isabelle couldn't have taken it," Ping whispered. "They're *good* people. They respect shoes-off-in-the-house traditions and they're polite to rude neighbours and they're just… nice!"

"Definitely not engagement ring thieves," Taptim agreed. "No way."

"We have to find it," Ping hissed. "Or your mum will fire Isabelle and we'll never see Clementine again."

Taptim's eyes widened. "We'll never learn how to make friendship bracelets. We'll never get Spark and Jelly to roll over."

Ping curled her hands into fists. "If only I had *noticed*."

"Never mind that!" Taptim rolled her eyes and jumped off her bed. "When they leave we'll check their bedroom and then work our way downstairs."

Once the car crunched away, Ping and Taptim crept into Uncle Jip and Aunty Lek's bedroom.

The babysitter was watching TV, so they tiptoed and whispered, probing behind pillows, burrowing under the bed and delving into dressing table drawers, their fingers feeling carefully between the contact lens boxes, the moisturisers and the handy packs of tissues. They went through Aunty Lek's coat and jacket pockets in the wardrobe, combed the carpet and inspected the inside of her handbags. Nothing.

They still hadn't found it when the babysitter came upstairs and told them to go to bed.

Ping couldn't sleep for ages. "Taptim," she said, "are you awake?"

"No," Taptim replied, making Ping grin.

"Let's get up really early and search tomorrow."

"Urgh."

At sunrise, Ping woke Taptim (it took a while), and as the others slept, they searched the stockroom. They looked under boxes, in boxes, behind furniture, under furniture, everywhere. No ring. They searched through every drawer and cupboard in the kitchen (and the fridge, just in case). They checked the bathroom. They searched the hallway, the shoe rack, the key basket. No ring.

Getting desperate and, unsurprisingly, quite hungry, they woke Tong, who wasn't impressed by being woken at 6am, and insisted he help them search. Which he did, to be fair, although Ping noticed he was not in the rosiest of moods. The three of them searched behind sofa cushions, inspected plant soil and looked under the lids of ornamental pots on high shelves. Places a ring could never have journeyed to unless it had a mind and powers of its own.

No ring.

When Aunty Lek came downstairs, Taptim and Ping had already been awake for two hours. Ping tried extremely hard to notice absolutely everything that morning to make up for not noticing the very important thing she really should have noticed yesterday. She noticed Aunty Lek was wearing a dark green T-shirt and her ring finger was bare. Ping noticed Aunty Lek's forehead was still knotted and her eyes were rimmed with red. And she noticed the mood in the house was as sombre as a slow march at a mournful parade.

"You don't need to keep searching," Aunty Lek said in a quiet voice. "I have a good idea where it is."

Ping wanted to ask a hundred and ten questions but she pursed her heart-shaped lips. Isabelle wasn't like that. She knew she wasn't. She couldn't be. Could she?

Taptim glared hard at Ping and then at her mother. "Do you really think Isabelle took it?"

Aunty Lek's eyes drifted and fixed on a distant stretch of sky beyond the window. "I don't know," she replied in a melancholy tone. "But I can't think of any other possibility."

"But she's so *nice*," Ping said, the bubbles bouncing but in a bad way. "She's not a thief."

"Thieves don't wear masks and carry swag bags, you know," Aunty Lek said, turning to Ping. "Sometimes good people do bad things when they're desperate."

Ping considered this. "Is Isabelle desperate?"

"Her husband's ill. They have financial problems at the moment. Look, I don't want to judge anyone – all I know is that my ring was here, and now it isn't. I'm going to call her and tell her not to come tomorrow. In fact, not come at all. Which is a shame because I need her help and I know she needs the job."

Ping's face flushed. She slowly shook her head at Taptim and bit the inside of her lip. Taptim did a *what can we do?* surrender gesture and poured herself a glass of water.

Aunty Lek took her phone into the storeroom and closed the door.

Ping tugged Taptim's arm, splashing water on the counter, and pulled her towards the storeroom door. They stuck their ears against it and heard Aunty Lek arguing. In traditional Thai style, she didn't fire words from her mouth with a *babababababababaa* like a machine gun volley, and she didn't raise her voice. She spoke quietly, calmly and firmly. When she stopped speaking, Ping and

Taptim jumped back from the door and scampered into the kitchen.

"What did she say?" Taptim asked casually, hiding the water splash with her flat hand.

"She insisted she didn't take it. She got upset. And then she got angry." Aunty Lek smoothed her lighter-than-before hair behind her ears and sighed. "But my ring was there, and now it's not. I have no other option but to fire her."

Ping's eyes brimmed with tears so she blinked hard. When they were safely blinked away, she mumbled, "But… what about Clementine?"

"Sorry. I know you like her but she won't be coming back. Now, I have to unpack all these boxes myself so I'll be busy this afternoon. You'll have to amuse yourselves."

Ping panicked. Surely… that couldn't be… it?

She had to think quickly. Luckily, an idea entered her fog-addled brain. It was a bit of an adventure-shaped idea, yes, but it was also *justice*-shaped, and *Clementine*-shaped, and those shapes were much more prominent. "Tong can take us to the park," Ping proposed. "Jelly needs a walk anyway."

"Great idea," Aunty Lek replied. She was still frowning. "You can take a picnic."

CHAPTER FIVE
THE SEARCH BEGINS

Tong wasn't overly delighted about taking them to the park. "Ughhh – do I have to?" he groaned in a gravelly growl, his voice high and then low, like an old car trying to start on a winter morning.

"Yes, Tong," Aunty Lek said. "You do."

"Yes, Tong," Ping repeated, flashing her eyes open again and again so he'd know she was trying to tell him something. "You do." Tong looked at her like she had an earthworm wriggling out of her nostril. He clearly didn't understand secret eye codes.

Taptim grinned. "What – not looking your best today?" she teased. "Worried you'll bump into your friends and you won't look cool?"

Ping faced him. She hadn't paid the slightest attention to how Tong looked today – or any

51

other day, for that matter – and that bothered her. Her senses should have been on high alert about absolutely everything at all times. Tong did seem paler and groggier than usual – but then that was no doubt their fault for waking him up so early. But why would he care about how he looked in the park? Why would *anyone* care?

Teenagers. So confusing.

Tong swept a hand through his hair and retorted. "I look awesome. As always. But I have to walk around outside with you two." He suddenly looked as if he was in pain. "And pick up Jelly's… deposits… in a plastic bag."

Ping laughed but then noticed that Tong wasn't joking. She opened her mouth, fully prepared to say that she would pick up Jelly's 'deposits', but then she closed it again because watching Tong doing it, cringing with embarrassment, would be much more fun.

"I need… things. For the park," Ping announced. She felt bad because adventures were very much out of the question and this was undeniably adventure-like, but she also felt excited because, well, this was undeniably adventure-like. She ran upstairs and packed a small backpack with her notebook, her magnifying glass, her paintbrush and a torch. She had no idea if she'd need the last three items but she put them in anyway. She needn't have rushed because twenty minutes later, Taptim was still looking in her bedroom mirror.

"Why are you taking all that… stuff?" Taptim asked, eyeing the backpack and picking up her earphones and her phone.

"Isabelle didn't steal that ring," Ping replied firmly. "I know she didn't. We have some detective work to do. You said you wanted a mystery to solve."

"Actually, I didn't. I said *Jelly* was an excellent detective dog. I didn't say–"

"So let's try him out."

Taptim scoffed. "He's not going to find an engagement ring, Ping. And anyway, I thought you weren't allowed any adventures."

Ping winced. It was a quandary, for sure. Her mother would be angry with her but in her quiet, graceful way. When her mother was angry, it was more like an infinitesimal ripple on a still lake than a mighty wave pummelling a coastal cliff. And what about the alpacas? Would she ever know whether her favourite preferred her to call him Mr Al Packington or Alberto Pacolito?

Ping was torn. Why was 'adventure' such a bad word anyway?

"This is definitely not an adventure," she said at last. "This is a… mission. Isabelle needs the job. We need to be friends with Clementine. And the world needs justice."

"*Kkkhhhh*." Taptim made a noise like a choking rattlesnake. "Really," she drawled. "You're doing this for world justice, are you? If you'd just said you were doing this for Isabelle and Clementine, I'd have said, 'I'm in'."

"But you *are* in, right?" Ping checked, "because I can't do this alone."

Taptim did a slow, hard blink, as if younger cousins who were not yet eleven were extremely bothersome. Then she sighed and said, "Fine. What's the plan?"

Ping opened her mouth to tell her but then Tong appeared at the door. "You two ready yet? How long can it take to—"

"Tong," Ping said, hooking her wayward hair behind her ears in an effort to seem efficient. She'd seen Aunty Lek do it but then Aunty Lek's hair didn't look like a dismantled birds' nest. "We need to retrace your mother's steps yesterday. Do you know the password to her phone? Not to… snoop or anything. Just to see her calendar."

"Pff!" Tong snorted. "That's exactly what snooping is. I'm not taking my mum's phone and searching through it. Do you think I'm *crazy*?"

"Not *take* it." Ping held up her notebook. "You only need to *peek* at it for one minute and write down where she was yesterday. Just so we can eliminate the other possibilities."

"Sometimes you don't need to eliminate other possibilities," Tong replied, dryly. "Sometimes the other possibilities are what actually happened."

"Please," Ping pleaded, her eyes stinging with the injustice of it all. "I believe in them. Can't we just make sure it isn't anywhere else?"

"Tong," Taptim said, turning away from the mirror at last. "She's got a point."

"I know her password," Tong said, rolling his eyes. "She gets me to text her customers when she's driving. You two distract her and I'll check her calendar. It's probably, like, against the law and I'll go to prison but hey, *you* believe in them and that's all that matters."

"What *is* it with his voice?" Ping asked when he left the room.

"It's breaking," Taptim said. "Happens to the male species around this age."

"Sounds like he's being strangled. Will it get better?"

"It will get *deep*," Taptim said in a cavernous voice. "And stay like that forever."

"Oh. Weird," Ping replied. "Will he still imitate a T-Rex and run around the garden trying to eat me?"

"I think those days might be over," Taptim replied, slipping her phone in her jacket pocket and zipping it up. "Let's go."

Distracting Aunty Lek was easy. Taptim hid Jelly's lead under the coats on the rack, so Aunty Lek had to hunt everywhere for it, and Ping and Taptim pretended to hunt with her. When Tong came out of the sitting room, he slid her phone back on the sideboard and winked at them. Aunty Lek was hunting through carrier bags in the kitchen, so Taptim reached for the coats, pulled them up and unhooked the lead. "Here it is!"

"What's it doing under there?" Aunty Lek asked in exasperation as she came into the hallway. "Honestly. Do you have some snacks and water, Tong? Good. It's a lovely day so take your time. Any problems call me and I'll come and pick you up. Taptim, do you have your phone?"

Course she does, Ping thought. *She's never off it.*

Ping didn't have a phone. When was she going to get one? And when she did, would she be glued to hers all the time as well? Because frankly it was a bit annoying.

"Don't use your entire battery listening to music because I might need to call you," Aunty Lek added. "Ping, stay with them at all times, OK?"

Ping nodded. She was excited about the detective work ahead but worried that if she didn't solve it, Isabelle wouldn't get her job back, they'd never see Clementine again and that would be that. Except with the added issues that Ping would be in big trouble, she wouldn't see the alpacas and she would probably never be allowed to stay with Taptim and Tong again in the holidays.

She tried not to think about that as they *crunch crunch crunched* out of the driveway, the monster eating a whole multipack of crisps. Once they were halfway down the road, near the oak where Spark liked to lift his leg, Ping asked Tong, "Right. Where did she go yesterday?"

Tong took out the notebook. "Can't believe I agreed to this," he grumbled. "Sooo... she went to her shop first, then the hairdressers, and then the bank. Then she met Yai for coffee and then she went home because you and your mum were coming over."

"Let's start at her shop, then," Ping said decisively.

Tong eyed Taptim and asked, "Why are we going along with this?"

"Because Ping's finally got a case to solve. And because they're not thieves," Taptim said, tonelessly. "All we need to do is prove it. I just hope we can."

CHAPTER SIX
THE PROCESS OF
ELIMINATION

The carved teak door of *Sukhothai* was open and Sue was behind the counter in a blue dress. Ping noticed that her long brown hair was tied up and she wore silver dolphin earrings. Ping also noticed she liked jewellery because she had lots of it on. Instinctively, Ping checked her hands for rings, and then felt bad for suspecting her.

Sukhothai was a grotto of wonder. Ping loved the handmade greetings cards, handicrafts and little people carved from wood. She adored the triangular cushions and paintings and furniture made of teak. She marvelled at it all, but she didn't have time to browse and choose what she'd have in *her* house. Not today.

"Hi Sue," Taptim said. "We've come to–" she stopped and coughed.

"We've come to look around," Ping said, taking over. "Just to, you know. Look. Around."

Sue seemed confused. "You've come to look around just to look around?"

Ping nodded, aware that it sounded odd but it was too late to backtrack now.

"At anything in particular?"

Tong came straight out with it. "Was my mum here yesterday?" he asked Sue. "And did she leave her engagement ring?" Ping shot him a look. This was not the way detectives worked. They were subtle and scheming and clever, not blunt. Or maybe being blunt was better and Ping had got it wrong this whole time.

"Oh, hasn't she found it yet? No, she came as I was opening up yesterday but she didn't take her ring off. She talked to me for ten minutes and then left. She rang me last night to ask if I'd seen it."

Ping clicked the top of her pen and wrote in her notebook: No ring. Talked to Sue for ten–

Taptim batted the book away. "You don't need to write that down," she hissed. "It's irrelevant. There's no ring here and no clues. Let's go."

The hairdressers, *Dyeing to Style*, was a twenty minute walk down the high street. Ping knew of other places called *Hair Today Gone Tomorrow*, *Shear Lock Combs*, and *Headward Scissorhands*. What was it about hairdressers and pun names?

"I'm not going in," Tong said, eyeing the black walls, the mock tiger skin sofa and the all-female clientele. "I'll wait here with Jelly."

"Fine," Ping said, then jostled Taptim in front of her towards the reception desk. There was plenty to notice about the receptionist. She wore a zebra-striped jumpsuit and her hair was dyed in black and white strips to match. Her nails were white with yellow tips and she had shimmer across her cheeks in pinky-silver stripes. She wore a small black stud in her thin, high nose and a badge in her lapel that read *I woke up like this*. Ping thought that waking up like that was not something she'd brag about personally, but she thought it best not to mention it.

Taptim scowled at Ping, then said politely, "Hello. My mother came in here yesterday at ten. Could we please have a word with the hairdresser who did her hair?"

"Dunt she like it?" the receptionist asked, chewing the end of her pencil.

"Oh, no, she loves it," Taptim lied. "We just need to ask her something."

The receptionist checked the appointment book. "Claudia did it. *CLAUDIA!*" she bellowed behind her. *"CLAUDIA!!!!"*

Ping and Taptim's eyes widened, and Tong, mortified, walked breezily away from the shop front with Jelly.

The person who had to be Claudia came out looking harassed. She hooked her fingers into the empty belt loops, hiked her jeans up, and snapped, "What?"

"Oh… hello," Ping said sweetly, despite being alarmed. "You did my Aunty Lek's hair yesterday. Did she leave a ring here by any chance?"

"People don't take rings off at the hairdressers, babe."

"But maybe it fell off?"

"Nah. We'd have seen it. But I'll keep my eye out, alright?"

Deflated, Ping mumbled, "Thank you."

Tong was across the paved road, standing outside a beauty salon. "Jelly pulled me over here," he said. "He's been sniffing like mad. I think he wants his legs waxed."

Ping grinned.

"Let me guess," Tong said. "No ring."

"No ring," Taptim confirmed.

They went to the bank. No ring. They went to the coffee shop. No ring. Taptim and Tong seemed a little grumpy. Maybe it was the teenage thing – Ping had seen programmes about teenagers on TV. Or maybe Taptim was missing her phone.

She hadn't looked at it for over fifteen minutes – anything could have happened in that time, but most likely, nothing had.

Tong scowled. "This is pointless. The only place she'd have taken it off is at home when she was cooking."

"But–" Ping said.

"No buts. Enough of this. We're going to the park."

The high street was full of interesting things to notice but inside her skull Ping was squeezing her brain like a sponge, trying to remember whether she'd seen the ring in the small bowl in the kitchen. She'd never tried as hard to picture anything as she was trying to picture that bowl. Why hadn't she noticed if the ring was in it? More worryingly, had she even noticed a *bowl*?

She felt a little panicky. They hadn't had any luck and the ring wasn't at home. Not anywhere they'd looked, anyway. "It's hard being a detective," she said to Taptim as they walked through the gates of the park. "How do you know what you're supposed to notice?" Ping shook her head. "We're missing something."

"Maybe we're not," Tong said, pulling Jelly away from a barking terrier. "Maybe Isabelle took it. And I have to spend a whole afternoon with you two."

"And Jelly," Taptim grinned. "And his poop."

Ping wanted to laugh but something was niggling her. "Isabelle told Clementine to be nice to their rude neighbours. And she made her take her shoes off in the house. They have respect for other people and their belongings. Someone like that would never steal!"

"Pah!" Tong replied. "There's no connection between people taking shoes off and stealing something valuable when they get the chance."

But Ping wasn't so certain. As they followed Jelly and his sniffing targets, she said, "I'm replaying the day backwards from when Isabelle and Clementine left. Just to cover everything. Let's sit here for a bit." She took out her notebook and pencil, and sat on a nearby bench. "The last thing they did was put their shoes on and the ring isn't near the shoes – we've looked. Before that, Isabelle filled her water bottle, and the ring isn't in the kitchen. And before *that*, they were in the stockroom."

"Looked there," Taptim said, sitting beside her.

"Let's look again. Diamond rings don't just disappear."

"Exactly," Tong said. "They get stolen."

"Not by nice people."

Tong's face looked like a seasick squirrel. "Whatever."

"Where was your mum before that?" Ping asked, scribbling notes in her pad.

"No idea," Taptim said, pulling her phone out. "We were in the garden. Listen, Ping, I'm only doing this because I like Clementine. Not because you think you're some kind of detective."

"I'm starving," Tong said, and took some sandwiches, a packet of popcorn and a box of crispy seaweed from his bag. He ate like he'd never seen food before, and Ping, still thinking, ate a sheet of seaweed. It tasted like salty tracing paper with sea seasoning.

"Was your mum wearing her ring when we had lunch?" Ping asked, swallowing.

"Didn't notice," Taptim said, not looking up from her phone.

"How could you not notice?" Ping screeched. "Some people don't notice *anything*."

"Did you?"

Ping winced. "No," she admitted. Great detective *she* was. "Where else could it be?"

"Nowhere," Tong said and popped some popcorn into his mouth. *Was that why it was called popcorn?* Ping wanted to ask, but it wasn't the time. "Mum's really careful with it – she wouldn't leave it lying around. Give up, Ping. This is boring."

Ping didn't want to give up but her resolve had more or less dissolved. Maybe she *was* wrong. Maybe Isabelle really had stolen it. But… Ping had a *feeling*.

What if her feeling was wrong?

Detectives had to be scrupulous and methodical and Ping wasn't either of those things, but she *was* as tenacious as a terrier, and that was going to get her much further in life, she was sure of it.

As some ominous grey clouds gathered, Ping gazed around the park at the frisbee players throwing frisbees, the dogs chasing balls, the joggers jogging and the walkers chatting. She hadn't noticed the one and only important thing she really should have noticed, and soon it would be time to go home. Aunty Lek would still have no ring. Isabelle would still have no job. And they'd never see Clementine again.

Missing the odd clue really did matter, after all.

On the plus side, Ping thought, *at least it hadn't rained yet.*

And then it started raining.

It was only a shower but they had to run under an awning until it passed. Ping listened to the hiss of the rain and watched as people ran for cover.

Taptim put her earphones in and Tong rubbed drops of rain off Jelly's back. By then it was nearly five and time to go home.

Start from the very very *beginning*, Ping told herself, closing her eyes. She cast her mind back to the moment she and her mother arrived at Aunty Lek's.

We pulled onto the gravel. The monster ate crisps. Aunty Lek opened the door. Had she been wearing her ring when she *wai*ed?

If only Ping had noticed.

Come on, brain, Ping thought, *what did you see?* Our car pulled in. Gravel. Car door. Monster eating crisps. Front door opened. *Wai*. Red jumper. Light hair.

"*Huugghhhttt!*" Ping jumped in a blast of heat, noise and energy. "I've got it!"

Taptim looked up from her phone.

"Got what?" Tong asked.

Ping grabbed Taptim's phone off her and Taptim pulled her earphones out, yelling, "Heyyy!"

"I think I know where it is. I'll tell you on the way," Ping yelled. "Come on! It's late and it'll be closing soon!"

CHAPTER SEVEN
THE LOST THING

Beyond the bottles of shampoo, Ping could see Claudia standing behind a chair. Her client was sitting in it leafing through a magazine, her wet spaghetti strands of hair tied loosely in clips. Claudia stopped snipping to hike her jeans up by the belt loops. *Why didn't she just buy the right size?* Ping wondered.

Ping didn't bother with the receptionist this time. She bolted in, far less calmly than her mother would have liked, and ran to Claudia.

"You again," Claudia said. "Told you already, she didn't–"

"She had her nails done!" Ping cried. "While she was waiting!"

"Oh, yeah, she did," Claudia said, "across the road. At *Beauty Bar*. The foils had to stay on for half an hour so she went to have a manicure."

And you didn't think of mentioning that? Ping wanted to yell, but instead she ran out shouting, "Thank you!"

"Genius!" Taptim yelled, high-fiving Ping.

"It wouldn't have been in her phone calendar because she did it on impulse," Ping said. "The ring has to be there!"

Beauty Bar was across the road, but there was one small problem. It was past five and the sign on the door said **Closed**. Jelly had been pulling Tong in that direction again anyway, so they followed him. As they crossed the paved street, Taptim said to Tong, "Didn't Jelly pull you this way earlier?"

Tong nodded as best he could, his arm being yanked by his frisky hound.

Taptim rapped at the door and said through the glass, "EXCUSE ME?"

She was getting into this now, Ping could tell.

"Closed," the woman mouthed from inside. She made an X with her arms just in case they didn't understand words.

Ping took over and yelled through the door. "MY AUNTY... SHE HAD A MANICURE YESTERDAY AND–" she gestured wildly as the woman seemed to be quite fluent in the language of arm movements. Ping thought she was doing well until Tong muttered, "You look like a malfunctioning wind-up toy."

"We're CLOSED," the woman repeated, opening her mouth as wide as a cavern. A sign above her on the wall said, '**Thieves will be prosecuted**'.

Ping gulped. *Prosecuted. Not a great word,* she thought, *under the circumstances.*

"PLEASE. DID SHE LEAVE HER RING?" Ping was not giving up. "HER RING!" She pointed at her finger and jabbed it a few times where a ring would be.

The woman at reception frowned, walked their way and unlocked the door. "Don't you know the meaning of the word 'closed'? Honestly, if I had a pound for every–"

"Sorry," Ping said. "But it's really important."

The woman sniffed indignantly. "I only started at three. I'll ask Mary."

She locked the door again and disappeared into the back.

Tong rubbed his hand across his entire face from top to bottom and muttered, "I should have stayed in bed this morning."

"I'm glad you didn't," Ping said. "You're a superhero."

Taptim snorted. "Him? Superhero? Sure."

"He is!" Ping snapped. "He came with us, didn't he? He checked your mum's phone and he got up early to help us search the house and he's not even moaning – not that much anyway. It has to be here. This is our last resort."

A young black woman with long hair and deep red lipstick came to the door. "Yes?" she said.

"I'm Mary, the owner. Can I help you?" Ping tried to explain but the words burst from her mouth in a blast of heat, noise and energy.

"Wait," Mary said, waving her hands. "Slowly."

Ping took a breath and explained as clearly as she could. "My aunty, Lek Bunnag, had a manicure here yesterday. She was at the hairdressers across the road so she would have had silver foil on her head."

"Oh, yes, I remember."

"Did she leave a ring here?"

Mary didn't say yes. But she didn't say no. "What kind of ring?" she asked.

Taptim said, "It's gold with a sapphire in the middle and a diamond each side. It's her engagement ring."

Mary's eyes glinted and she said, "One sec." She closed the door on them and Tong, Ping and Taptim glanced at each other. Ping peered through the window and watched Mary walk behind the reception desk, open a drawer and take out an envelope. She held it up and Ping's stomach flipped.

Taptim muttered, "Do you think she knows that's an envelope and not a ring?"

Mary opened the door again, and said, "You're in luck." She opened the envelope so they could see inside. Aunty Lek's engagement ring lay in the fold at the bottom.

Ping and Taptim yelled, "YESSSS!" and hugged each other, laughing.

"Wow," Tong said, making a face. "I really didn't think–"

"She *didn't* steal it!" Ping cried. "I KNEW it!"

"*Me?*" Mary seemed offended. "Course I didn't steal it! We didn't know who left it here so we put it away hoping they'd come back."

Taptim gasped. "Sorry – no, not you! My mother thought someone *else* stole it – someone who came to visit us yesterday. Thank goodness you've got it!"

Mary looked relieved. "I put it in our Lost Property drawer. I phoned everyone in the appointment book but some clients just walk in and we don't have their phone number. We'd never have known it was hers unless she'd remembered and come back. Can she come and collect it? I'd give it to you but I don't want you to lose it."

"We wouldn't," Ping insisted. "We'd—"

"Absolutely not. We'd be really careful," Taptim added.

"I believe you, honest I do, but it's valuable so I'd rather give it to her in person. I can wait if she comes now."

Tong took his mobile phone out. "*Mair krup,*" he said, using the Thai name for 'Mother', "we're at the beauty salon. Your ring is here. You left it here when you had your nails painted. The shop's closed but the owner said if you come now, she'll wait for you."

Tong put his phone in his pocket and smiled. "She'll be here in ten minutes."

At that moment Jelly barked, making Mary jump. Ping bent down and rubbed his ears. "Good *boy*, Jelly," she said. "You were trying to tell us, weren't you? You must have smelled Aunty Lek's scent."

"Shame we don't speak Beagle," Taptim said.

"You'd better come in," Mary said, opening the door. "Looks like it might rain again." In the reception area, she gave Jelly some water, and chatted to Tong, Ping and Taptim as rain streaked the windows and Tong tried to keep Jelly away from the equipment.

When Aunty Lek arrived, she looked pale and very sheepish. She thanked Mary profusely, and on the way home in the car said, "Thank goodness for Ping. I'm so embarrassed. I was sure... oh, I feel terrible for suspecting Isabelle. I have to call her and apologise."

CHAPTER EIGHT
TWO-LEGGED FRIENDS
AND
FOUR-LEGGED FRIENDS

Ping heard a crunching on the gravel. Aunty Lek opened the door and Ping noticed the long green estate car with the light blue door pulling onto the driveway.

Isabelle got out, but Clementine and Spark stayed in the car.

Ping tried to notice everything now. She noticed Tong was being nicer to her, probably because he'd been wrong and she'd been right. She noticed Taptim was holding Jelly's lead in one hand and for once, her phone wasn't in the other. She noticed Aunty Lek's engagement ring was on her finger, and that she walked towards Isabelle's car with her head hanging low and a solemn expression on her face.

"I can't tell you how sorry I am." Aunty Lek wrung her hands nervously as she approached Isabelle. "I'm so embarrassed and ashamed. Please forgive me. I completely understand if you don't want to work with me, but you have your job back if you'd like it. Either way, please have lunch with us and let me make amends."

Ping noticed that Isabelle wasn't smiling, her whole body seemed stiff, and her jaw was jutting out. She noticed the hurt hanging in the air and the way Isabelle's body seemed to push away from Aunty Lek, like one magnet repelling another.

"Under normal circumstances," Isabelle replied, coldly, "I wouldn't want to have lunch with you. I wouldn't have come over at all. How could you think I'd do something like that?" She shook her head. "You really hurt me, Lek."

Ping noticed that the atmosphere had become even more awkward. Tong stared fixedly at the ground. Taptim did, too. Clementine stayed in the car, sitting very still, looking at the oak and not at them. And Aunty Lek's eyes welled up. She replied so quietly, Ping could barely hear, "I... I didn't know what else to think. I just... I made a terrible mistake, Isabelle, and I'm so, so sorry."

Ping bit her lip in alarm. She hadn't thought this far ahead. She hadn't taken hurt feelings or embarrassment into account. She'd thought that once she'd found the ring, everything would go back to normal and they'd all be happy, but as it was, only the dogs were happy. Spark was wagging his tail, panting, inside the car, and Jelly was barking with excitement.

After what seemed like an eternity, Isabelle sighed. She shuffled her feet and Aunty Lek swallowed, her head still low and her hands still clasped together.

"That said," Isabelle added, "I'm not the sort of person to hold grudges. Everyone makes mistakes."

Aunty Lek looked up at her hopefully, but Ping noticed she couldn't speak as she was trying very hard not to cry.

"Anyway," Isabelle added, "Clementine loved playing with the girls, and I… well, I'm a sucker for your food." She smiled, held out her hand to Aunty Lek and said, "Apology accepted."

Aunty Lek shook Isabelle's hand, and wiped her eyes. "If I make you food every day for a week, will you consider working with me again?"

Isabelle paused, then said with a half-smile. "I'll think about it. Clementine, you can come out."

Clementine and Spark crunched across the gravel towards Ping, Taptim and Tong, and all of them walked towards the house, which sounded to Ping like the monster was enjoying a multipack of multipacks of crisps.

Clementine stepped *over* the threshold this time. She levered off her shoes with her toes, whispering, "Phew! I didn't think I'd see either of you again."

"Nor did we," Taptim said with a grin. "It's all thanks to Ping."

"And Jelly," Ping added, rubbing Jelly's head, even though she knew it really was all thanks to her.

The three of them ran through the kitchen and out of the patio doors to the garden. Tong came along too, for a change. Jelly and Spark went on a sniffing expedition of the garden, and Taptim and Clementine sat in the summer house, talking. *Probably about their phones,* Ping thought, rolling her eyes.

She went to stand opposite Tong with her hands on her hips. "*Pleeeeease,*" she pleaded.

"No way."

"*Please!*"

"Uh-uh."

"For old times' sake."

Tong sighed and growled, "Fine." And he imitated a T-Rex and chased Ping around the garden trying to eat her.

*

At the end of the week, when Ping's mum Chabah came to collect Ping, she said, "I hear you had quite an adventure."

Ping noticed her mother didn't look very happy about it. She also noticed that even though she was wearing a white shirt and beige trousers, and not her silk dress, she still looked as if she were performing a mesmerising dance when she unbuttoned her jacket.

Ping twisted her lips. "Err… yeeeesssss… But I didn't *mean* to…"

Her mother smiled. "Ping Ping, you used your head, found Aunty Lek's ring, and fixed a very tricky situation. Perhaps adventures aren't *all* bad, am I right?"

Relieved, Ping nodded.

"As a reward," Ping's mum added, "this is what I suggest we do."

*

The following weekend, Ping, Taptim and Clementine climbed into the back of Chabah's car. Tong had politely declined the invitation, claiming he had school work to do, but Ping thought he was probably just being a bit of a teenager.

On the way there, the girls compared their new friendship bracelets, sang along to the radio (out of tune), and were so excited and squealy that three times on the way, Chabah turned her head, frowning a little, and murmured, "Shh, shh, Ping. Please be calm, OK?"

When they reached the farm, Ping tried not to shriek, though her throat wanted to. She tried not to jump up and down, though her body wanted to. And she tried not to sprint to the fence with her arms windmilling, though her legs and arms wanted to. She ran as close as she could to her favourite brown alpaca with a tuft of curls on his head, huge brown eyes and long eyelashes. "There he is!" she said, pointing to him.

"He's sweeeet!" Clementine squealed.

"I love them all!" Taptim cried, looking around. Fifteen or so were dotted around the field, dark and white ones, all with ringlet curls between their ears and enormous gentle eyes. Taptim pulled out her phone to take selfies, and Ping rolled her eyes. Then she jumped in front of the lens with her thumbs up.

As the three of them gazed fondly at Ping's favourite brown alpaca, Ping asked Clementine, "How will I know which name he likes best?"

Clementine thought for a moment. "He'll give you a sign," she answered, confidently.

"What kind of sign?"

Clementine shrugged. "You'll know when you see it."

"OK," Ping said, hoping Clementine was right.

Ping cleared her throat. She felt a bit odd, doing this, but there was no way around it. "Mr Al Packington?" she tested in a loud, clear voice.

The alpaca looked blankly at her with his chocolatey eyes. His mop crop of curly hair made her heart melt. She wished she could take him home and keep him in the back garden.

"Alberto Pacolito?" she tried.

The alpaca started making a cute, buzzing hum. Almost like a cat's purr. He hummed some more. Then he turned his head, ripped a mouthful of straw from his bale, and chewed.

Ping laughed. "Alberto Pacolito it is," she said.

One of her arms linked with Clementine's and the other linked with Taptim's, then with springs in her shoes, bubbles in her body, and roars and giggles and yells trying to leap free from her lungs to the tips of the trees, Ping waved goodbye to Alberto Pacolito, and the three of them skipped happily towards the farm café.

READING ZONE!

QUIZ TIME

Can you remember the answers to these questions?

- What is the name of Ping's mother?

- Why do many Thai people step over the threshold and not on it?

- Where does Aunty Lek always put her ring when she is cooking?

- How does Tong know his mother's passcode for her phone?

- How does Ping know which name to call her favourite alpaca?

READING ZONE!

STORYTELLING TOOLKIT

The author introduces us to lots of different characters during the story.

Can you write short descriptions of your three favourite characters? Note down what they look like, what their personality is like and how they behave, using the text to help you.

READING ZONE!

GET CREATIVE

The book features a mystery that Ping has to solve. Have you read other mystery stories where children are the detectives?

Can you plan and then write another mystery story for Ping to solve? Decide what goes missing, where it ends up and how Ping will find it. Use the structure of this book to help you.